MR. GEORGE

— AND THE —

RED HAT

Written and Illustrated by
STEPHEN HEIGH

Edited by
KEVIN BURTON

KRBY Creations, LLC
Bay Head, New Jersey

ISBN 0-9745715-2-0
Library of Congress Control Number: 2004092864

Printed and Bound in China

Editor and Publisher:
Kevin R. Burton
KRBY Creations, LLC
Post Office Box 327
Bay Head, NJ 08742
www.KRBYCreations.com

Dedicated to
Ania, Thomas, and Anna
With Love

Mr. George is a friendly little squirrel who lives in a park. The park looks just like one near you, with trees and walking paths. Some parts of the park have grass and others are covered with bushes. The park is filled with animals, like birds and rabbits, and squirrels like Mr. George.

One day, while on his way to collect
acorns and peanuts, Mr. George
found a small doll hat made of
bright red felt. It was just lying on
the ground at the foot of a tree,
and Mr. George thought it was the
prettiest hat he had ever seen.

Mr. George was curious. "Where did the hat come from?" thought Mr. George.

At first he thought it could be a rabbit's hat. But then he wondered, "How could a rabbit with such tall ears wear a hat?"

Then Mr. George thought, "Maybe it's a groundhog's hat."

But no, what would a groundhog do with a hat? It wouldn't fit their large round head and the groundhog would surely get it dirty going underground.

"Could it belong to a chipmunk?"

No Way! It would completely
cover a chipmunk. Mr. George
laughed.

Mr. George thought long and hard about what kind of animal could use such a hat. An animal could use it to hold food that it picked up to save for another time to eat. It would have to be an animal that has short ears and a small head. The animal would have to be very smart and think about these things. "Who could use this hat?" thought Mr. George.

Mr. George thought and thought. He decided to put the hat on his head while he thought. It fit him perfectly.

Then, Mr. George looked at his reflection in a stream. "That's it!" thought Mr. George when he saw himself in the stream. This hat was meant for him.

WOW! A red hat for Mr. George.

Mr. George wore the hat all spring.
He took the hat wherever he went.
When he went looking for food,
Mr. George would gather acorns
and peanuts, and put them in his
hat to carry them.

Mr. George would climb a tree and hang his hat upside down from a branch and have a picnic in the tree. He could see the whole park under the bright blue sky.

Mr. George had lots of animal friends in the park. They all loved seeing Mr. George in his beautiful red hat.

There were the rabbits, the chipmunks, the raccoons, and the skunk, some mice and a frog, and even a turtle. They would all gather around Mr. George while he wore the red hat.

When summer arrived, Mr. George
heard from the other animals that
a new mother bird was looking for
a home for her family.

When he heard someone needed
a home, Mr. George had an idea.
He went off to find the young
mother bird.

It didn't take long for Mr. George to find her. With goodness in his heart, Mr. George gave his hat as a gift to the new mother bird. He told her it would make a fine new home for her family.

The mother bird hung the red hat
from a tree, and in it made a safe,
warm nest for her little baby birds.
It did indeed make a beautiful
home for the newborn family.

All the animals in the park cheered
for Mr. George and his kindness.
They showered him with wildflowers.
Mr. George was a wonderful friend
and neighbor to everyone in the
park. Maybe some day you will see
Mr. George, who gave his red hat
to the bird family.

∞ The End ∞